Albie's Trip
to the
Jumble Jungle

*Dedicated to Lee, Laura, and Andy and to
the wondrous imaginations of all children.* —R.S.

To my godmother, Aunt Carolyn Biner. —J.M.

A Jumble Jungle Book

TRICYCLE PRESS
a little division of Ten Speed Press
P.O. Box 7123
Berkeley, California 94707

Library of Congress Cataloging-in-Publication Data

Skutch, Robert.
Albie's trip to the Jumble Jungle / Robert Skutch;
illustrations by Joseph Mathieu.
p.   cm.
"A Jumble Jungle book."
Summary: Albie visits the Jumble Jungle and meets such
strange animals as a crocosmile, a flyon, and a forkupine.
ISBN 1-58246-076-0
[1. Animals--Fiction.] I. Mathieu, Joseph, ill. II. Title.
PZ7.S62873 Al 2002   [E]--dc21   2001006429

Printed in Singapore
1 2 3 4 5 6 - 05 04 03 02

Albie's Trip
to the
Jumble Jungle

by Robert Skutch

Illustrated by Joe Mathieu

A Jumble Jungle Book

TRICYCLE PRESS
Berkeley • Toronto

"There's a jungle show coming to town, Albie.
Would you like to go?" his father asked.
   "Nahh," Albie answered. "I've seen all the
animals on TV."

"Well, it's up to you," his mother said. "But your TV time is up. Take Tugs for a walk before dinner."

Albie and Tugs hadn't gone far before they came to a wooded area. A sign said...

"This must be the jungle show Dad talked about. Let's go in, Tugs."

As they started down the path, they saw another sign...

Name one animal correctly and win a **LIFETIME MEMBERSHIP** to the **Jumble Jungle**

"That'll be easy," Albie said.

They hadn't gone far when Albie heard
something crawling through the leaves.
"Look, Tugs, there's a crocodile."
"Nope!" the animal announced.
"Then what are you?" Albie asked.
"I'm a...

crocoSMILE!"

And with that, her face lit up, and she croaked:

"Though folks don't think much of my cousins,
And creeping is part of my style;
Still I'm really a friendly old critter,
You can tell by the size of my smile!"

And she crawled away, calling, "Beware of the kangarshoes!"

Before Albie could ask why, the crocosmile was gone, and another animal poked his head out of the bushes, and called, "You think you know all the animals, Albie? Then what am I?"

"You're a lion, of course," Albie answered.

" 'fraid not!" the animal growled. "Isn't it obvious? I'm a...

And then he roared:

"My cousin is king of the forest;
He's master of all he can see.
By flying, I see more than he does,
So I'm much more important than he!"

And away he flew.

"Wow!" Albie shouted, just as three animals appeared, somersaulting toward him. "Now I'm going to win that membership," he said. "You are polar bears!"

"Not quite," they answered gleefully. "We're...

ROLLER bears!"

Then they began singing:

"*Everywhere we go, we roll;*
We even roll up stairs.
We roll in snow, we roll in sleet;
That's why they call us Roller bears!"

And down the hill they rolled.

As he and Tugs headed for the Jumble Jungle gate, Albie stopped and looked. "You're an elephant, aren't you?" he asked hopefully.

"Ordinary thinking!" the animal replied, shaking her head. "I'm an...

To the
**Jumble
Jungle**
Gate

e**PLANT!**"

"But you're eating your trunk," Albie said with amazement. And the eleplant explained:

*"Because I'm a vegetarian
I nibble on trees frequently;
I'm never concerned about finding food,
For I grow my own dinners, you see.*

"You'd better not let the kangarshoes get you," she called before turning away.

A few steps further along the path they came across a little animal.

"Are you leaving without winning your membership?" it asked.

Albie hesitated. "Not if you're a porcupine," he said wishfully.

"Better try again! Can't you see I'm a...

FORKupine!"

And then he grunted:

*"I don't mind it when people first see me
If they smile and they start in to gawk.
For their smiles quickly turn into wonder
When they see that I eat with a fork!"*

"I guess we won't get that membership, Tugs," Albie said sadly. "But at least we didn't meet up with the kangarshoes." And with that...

To **Jumble Jungle** Gate

...two kangarshoes jumped into the path, blocking his way.

"Uh-oh," Albie whispered. Then he asked, "Why did they tell us to watch out for you?"

The kangarshoes shrugged, and one announced:

"We really are jolly old fellows;
Other animals we don't abuse.
We don't mean to cause any trouble,
We just like collecting old shoes!"

Then they grabbed Albie's sneakers, and began hopping away.

But before they could get very far...

...two striped animals blocked their way, and Albie rescued his sneakers. "Come on," one of his new heroes said, "we'll take you to the gate."

But when they got there, Albie couldn't open it. "The gate is locked," he said.

"Not to worry," one of the striped animals answered, as it moved toward the gate.

Albie let out a whoop and excitedly yelled, "You must be...

"Indeed we are," and they happily replied:

"Our job is important . . . to lock up the gate,
So strangers don't picnic and leave all their mess.
We know whom to welcome, and who to keep out;
That's surely the key to our brilliant success!"

"Albie," his mother said, "you were supposed to take Tugs for a walk."

"But I did, Mom."

"I didn't hear you go out," she replied.

"We went to a new place, Mom. We saw all kinds of different animals. And the great thing is, I can see them any time I want! Look...," he said, as he handed her a piece of paper.

Lifetime
membership
to the
Jumble
Jungle

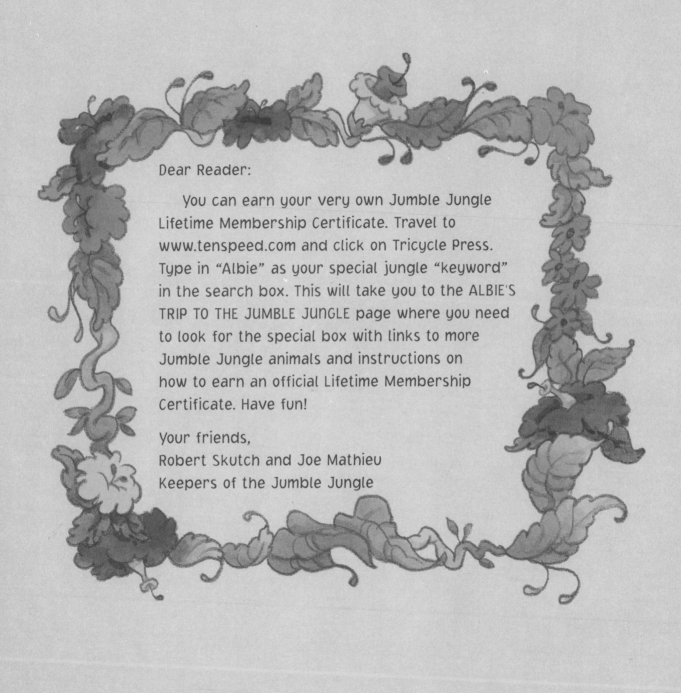

Dear Reader:

　　You can earn your very own Jumble Jungle
Lifetime Membership Certificate. Travel to
www.tenspeed.com and click on Tricycle Press.
Type in "Albie" as your special jungle "keyword"
in the search box. This will take you to the ALBIE'S
TRIP TO THE JUMBLE JUNGLE page where you need
to look for the special box with links to more
Jumble Jungle animals and instructions on
how to earn an official Lifetime Membership
Certificate. Have fun!

Your friends,
Robert Skutch and Joe Mathieu
Keepers of the Jumble Jungle